NONE OF US WILL BE OKAY

Liza Costello lives in the Irish midlands. Her poems, essays and stories have appeared in various magazines and newspapers, and have been broadcast on RTÉ Radio 1. She came first in the Dromineer Literary Festival Poetry Award, and was shortlisted for both the Patrick Kavanagh Award for an unpublished collection of poetry and the Francis MacManus Short Story Award. She has also written two novels.

Also by Liza Costello

Crookedwood   (Hachette, 2023)

The Estate   (Audible, 2020; Hachette, 2021)

CONTENTS

ISBN: 978-1-917617-53-6

Cover designed by Aaron Kent

Cover image: © harlequin9 / Adobe Stock

Edited by Alice Brooker

Typeset by Aaron Kent

Broken Sleep Books Ltd
PO BOX 102
Llandysul
SA44 9BG

For my parents

None of Us Will Be Okay

Liza Costello

Broken Sleep Books

THE STRANGLER TREE

Lurching down the dust road labyrinth of Guatemala, past the burnt meadows and frightening precipices, Padraig finally understood her idea that travel could cure all pain. He stepped over the basket of piglets at his feet, raw in their new wrinkled skin. He burrowed through the people-filled bus and climbed the ladder at the rear. He dropped his plan to give it a week before ending the trip. He was going to play this country by ear.

On the roof, every sharp turn had him holding his breath, then catching it. He grinned back when the other men up there, all locals, laughed. If he was not holding the bar when they reeled around a corner or plunged through a deep pothole, that could be it. Dead man tumbling. He let go a couple of times, just for the jolt. Once it came close and this time, the men did not laugh. They said things in this language he did not understand. They gesticulated with their free hands.

All day, the roadside was a hemline of litter to the sky and the mountains and the valleys. By the time he joined a young couple standing at the edge of a darkening village, there was dust in his eyelashes and on his teeth.

'You think our lift will show?' asked the male, blonde half.

'Doesn't look good,' said Padraig. He imagined knocking on the low doors of the houses made from wood and corrugated iron. Sleeping on the ground beneath one of those animal shelters with no walls. Listening to the rustle of unseen insects.

But the pickup came. On the snarling descent to the lake, the wind sang a mean song through his shirt but he did not follow suit when the couple dug into their backpacks, wrapped themselves in blankets.

'Aldous Huxley called it the most beautiful lake in the world,' shouted the male. Overhead the stars burned and glimpses of lake appeared, its borders announced by the dying bonfires of villages.

In the empty dining room of the hostel, they dined on yam and fried fish and terrible beer. The couple told Padraig about their trip around the world. Their names were Henk and Darya, and they were from the Netherlands.

'How about another beer?' said Padraig, when they had finished eating.

'You're not tired?' said Henk. 'I guess it's true what they say about the Irish.'

'Our boat's at five, isn't it?' said Padraig. '"Hardly seems any point in going to bed.'

'Sorry Padraig,' said Henk.

'I can't keep my eyes open,' said Darya.

In his bedroom, a spider the size of a small mouse scurried from underneath the bed when Padraig turned on the lamp. It paused in the centre of the room and he threw a book at it, but the spider just flashed back across the floor, disappearing again under the bed. Padraig pulled the bed into the centre of the room. This time, he did not see the spider run anywhere.

In bed, he tucked in the sheet all around him, so that even his head was covered. The air was warm and never felt like enough. An urge kept rising in him to clap his hands together, to frighten the spider away. He imagined Henk coming in to investigate, finding him there like a corpse, applauding alone. A bark of laughter escaped him. It echoed in the high ceilinged room.

In the silence that followed, Emily came to him. He could see the slight oiliness of her skin, the way she used to tilt her head when she looked at him, her wide gaze.

He closed his eyes. He tried not to think.

They had met at a birthday dinner for a mutual friend.

'This is Emily,' announced the friend on Padraig's arrival, and he indicated the empty seat beside her for Padraig to sit in. 'An artist from America, only came to Florence two months ago. A new expat for you. I get tired of talking to Padraig,' he continued, looking at Emily. 'Three years in Italy and he refuses to learn Italian. All the time, I translate for him. You two can talk together, yes?'

They were seated at the end of a long table. Padraig took in her fine brown hair pulled loosely from a small, beautiful face. He wanted to run his finger down her ruler sharp nose.

'This must be the most obvious set up I've ever found myself on,' she said, looking at her menu.

'You'll get used to that carry on here.'

'I was in Ireland once.' She glanced at him. 'I stayed on Achill Island. I didn't want to leave.'

'You picked a good spot,' he said, 'though beauty doesn't always run deep. Religion and greed aren't exactly ideal features in a country's makeup, if you're asking me.'

'It's the most pagan place I've ever been.'

'Really?'

'I met the parish priest. An atheist if ever I saw one.' She looked at him and laughed. He began to laugh himself.

'You may be onto something there.'

They were both in their late forties. Both childless, they also learned, with mutual, undisguised pleasure.

'At least I had a stab at marriage,' she said. 'At least I had a go.'

A few weeks later, walking back to his apartment with a bag of dinner ingredients, he broke off a large plum tomato from its stem and bit into it, as though it was an apple. She laughed, as he knew she would. She laughed like a child. Then she wrapped an arm around his neck and kissed him.

'Stop that,' she said, as he turned it into a French kiss and attempted to pass a chunk of un-chewed tomato into her mouth. She pulled herself away.

'I love you,' she said then. Her hand went to her mouth. 'I didn't know I was going to say that.'

'I love you too,' he said.

Padraig ended up spending two weeks in the hostel. In the evenings, he drank and smoked pot with whoever was around. During the day, he went on solitary hikes to neighbouring villages, as far as twelve miles on one occasion. When dogs came at him, their throaty snarls rippling through ketchup-red gums, he shook his stick at them. Sometimes he just kept walking. Once, a man clanged a machete on the side of the truck he had caught a ride home in, all the while shouting at the driver. Probably angry because he hadn't got the fare. Long, thin, blunt weapons. All the men had one. He thought of getting one for himself.

By the time Henk read out the description from his guidebook of Semuc Champey, natural wonder of the jungle, there was nowhere left to walk. It was Padraig who figured out the nearest village and the bus route to it and how long the journey would take. Henk and Darya decided to go too, along with a couple of newly arrived Israeli guys, and a girl called Céline. Beautiful, French Céline whose boyfriend had dumped her, two weeks into a trip they'd been planning for over a year.

'Is like this Padraig,' she said, speaking of her own broken heart. She purred his name. *Pawrg*. He had no intention of correcting her. 'With life, you have to keep moving. It doesn't care what you do, but it's better for you this way.'

They reached the village on the edge of the jungle just before the bottom of an angry red sun touched the horizon. Beds were provided in the first house they approached, and the following morning, they caught a lift with a Guatemalan tour group.

It was an old US school bus; halfway to their destination, on the steepest part of the road, it gave up. They were all to get off, they were told. Walk until the road grew flatter.

Before Padraig could catch up with the others, Henk positioned himself beside him. He began to talk about the landscape.

'Look at that tree,' he said, many words later.

The only thing remarkable about this tree, as far as Padraig could tell, was the pale grey colour of the trunk. But Henk had stopped walking.

'Notice anything unusual?'

'I don't. A bit hard looking maybe. Funny colour.'

Ahead, Céline was walking beside a Guatemalan woman, who was pulling a leaf from a tree. She gave it to Celine who tasted it, laughed, said something.

'It's not the real tree.' Henk spoke as though he had made it himself.

'Not following.'

'What you see is not the real tree. It's a parasite. They call it a strangler tree.'

Padraig resumed walking. 'Sounds a bit morbid.'

'A monkey or squirrel brings up the seed onto the old tree,' said Henk. 'Then a root grows, reaches the ground and the new tree begins. When the old one dies, the inside is like a cave.'

He started seeing them everywhere, wondered how he had not noticed them before – you only had to scan the bush a moment to spot yet another. It was the reason he glimpsed the mansion, nestled, half hidden, against the sulking green.

'What's a house doing out here?' he said, and he called the others. Together they walked down to it, its walls a now pale salmon, the shutters a pastel green. They peered through the letter box, and through cracks in the boarded up windows. They calculated at least ten rooms.

'That would make a pretty cool hostel,' said someone.

'Maybe I'll turn it into one.' He threw it out in the guise of a joke but Céline turned and stared at him.

'You fucking should Pawrg. That is exactly what you should do.'

For the rest of the walk and the three hours that followed on the recovered bus, it was all he thought about. They knew the destination was popular with Guatemalan tour groups. Why not make it popular with Western ones? He could organise private tours. He could open a bar out the back where people could watch the sunset while drinking mojitos. Renovating the place would be a huge challenge, just what he needed. He had heard some scary stories about local farmers driving away such Western ventures, but these were probably exaggerations. Anyway, there were ways of working with people. One thing he'd learned was that everyone wanted something. Maybe Céline was right, he thought, as the exhausted bus pulled to a halt. Maybe he fucking should do it.

The day he moved into Emily's apartment, it rained. All week, the sun had shone and only wimpy little white clouds crossed the sky. But on that day, a sky-wide grey hurled itself onto the city of Florence. He didn't have an umbrella. When she finally opened the door, rain had reached every part of him – his hair and face, his skin all over his body, even through his socks and underwear. It had probably reached his clothes in his rucksack. The daffodils he held clung wetly to his jacket, one of the stems broken.

Her face looked stretched, as though someone was standing behind her and pulling her hair. Leaving the door open, she walked down the hall and up the spiral staircase that led to her studio.

He placed the box on a sideboard in the hall. Followed her up there, towards the sounds of her flip flops slapping the wooden floor, things being lifted and put down again.

'I cannot bear this weather.'

'You don't get rain in Vermont, I suppose?'

No answer. He stayed on the stairs and waited. He had seen the size of the wooden beams she used to support her canvas.

When silence finally came, and he opened the door to the studio, he found her sitting on the ground with her back against the wall. She was staring at the skylight of still-raining sky. She kept staring at it when he crossed the room and sat down beside her.

'Sorry,' she said, after a good half hour had passed. Her voice could barely scrape the word out.

'If you don't want to do this,' his voice began. He thought of the daffodils downstairs.

When she turned to him, she was wearing that wry smile of hers.

It clashed with her smashed looking eyes.

'Aren't *you* frightened?' she said.

'No.'

It was an honest answer. Apparently, only five months had passed since they met. That was according to other people, to the calendar in his diary. But he was having trouble remembering a time when he did not know her.

The side of her head met his shoulder. She took his hand. He felt her lips on his palm.

Less than three years later, she was the one to move, to a hospice you could walk to from the apartment.

'You will get beyond this,' she said, in one of her final moments of lucidity.

'It's not about *me* getting beyond this.'

'Don't do that.'

More than the words, her tone of voice silenced him.

A chain of turquoise pools shimmered across the tangled green of bush and trees. At the top of the waterfall that began the whole thing, Padraig watched the others splashing in the first pool, oblivious to his new status of watcher. A howler monkey roaring from somewhere behind him, he waved and waved until Céline looked up and waved back.

The rocky ledge was warm from the sun; carefully he eased himself into a sitting position, his legs swinging like a child on an adult's chair. The noise of the water leant an air of urgency to the moment and wouldn't let his gaze rest anywhere else. It threw itself white and spraying onto the rocks below.

It wasn't a sharp drop. At least, not as sharp as he first conclud- ed. Another ledge lay below him, and after it, two other rocks jutted out. If a person was very careful, they could climb down all the way to the bottom. It was practically as straightforward as the way he climbed up, on the other side.

If he pulled this off, it would be a sign. He would go ahead with the hostel. Stomach-down on the grass, he swivelled himself around, until his feet hung in the air. Then, hands clutching at the weedy grass, he began to lower himself. His left hand was beginning to slip by the time his feet met rock. He heard his voice cry out.

'Thank fuck,' it said, barely audible against the crashing water.

Rapid heartbeats drummed inside him. A couple of minutes passed before he could look down. Now he was there, he realised the ledge was thinner than he initially believed. But once he was lying on it, stomach-down again, he should be able to slide onto the first rock below. Even if he fell from there, chances were he would not do much damage.

The fall happened without his realising it was going to. He hadn't even begun to swing himself around when he was sliding, and then, for the briefest moment, airborne. When he opened his eyes, Henk was standing over him. Pain struck from his left elbow and he could taste blood.

'Sorry,' he said, in a hoarse voice. As he spoke, he felt something hard and pointed underneath his tongue. He fished out a fragment of tooth. Running his tongue over his teeth he discovered a jagged edge on one of the front ones.

'What were you thinking?' said Henk, taking Padraig's left hand in his own and stretching out his arm until a yelp escaped him.

'Broken,' said Henk.

'You are an extremely lucky man,' said Darya, who looked bored by the whole thing.

'Were you trying to fucking kill yourself?' said Céline.

Henk made a sling and Céline gave him painkillers. He would get a lift back to the village from the first tour group that came. It was holiday season in Guatemala; there would probably be one the following day. No one asked what he would do after that. He went to his tent before dinner. Later, Céline brought him a glass of wine.

'Here you are, show-off,' was all she said before ducking out again.

The next morning, pain woke him, his elbow aching and lower lip throbbing fatly. He sat up. He went outside. Walked past the dead fire, the three other tents on the other side, all zipped shut. He walked into the cluster of trees at the water's edge.

Ahead, a large freckle of sunlight stained the ground. He would walk to it and back, he decided. On his way, he could gather firewood to make coffee.

Before he reached the sunlight, he came across the strangler tree. It was bigger than the other trees there and a wider space surrounded it than any of them. Padraig walked right up to it. Stroked the pale, grey bark that seemed hard as metal. Peering inside a small gap he found at the back, he waited for his eyes to adjust to the deeper darkness, but a sour smell rose up to greet him and his head pulled back. It was impossible to tell how much of what was in there was the dead, original tree and how much was cavity. He put his eye to the gap again but the sound of eager scuffling had him jerking back a second time. A rat perhaps, or a large insect. Maybe even a snake. It stopped as quickly as it started.

At the very end, she didn't know who he was. She did not know who anyone was. The cancer had reached her brain and that, along with the morphine, made her look out at them all with those furious, uncomprehending eyes. Life goes on, people said to him. You have to get on with it. It's what she would have wanted. You can't give up.

The scuffling started again. This time it sounded closer to the gap, as though something inside was crawling its way forward. He took a step backwards and turned around. Started to make his way back to where the others were.

COLETTE WENT QUIET

The phone startled me when it buzzed awake on the counter top, late in the day I moved into my apartment. For hours, I had been carrying boxes from my car, wiping down the insides of cupboards and wardrobes, slicing my penknife through duct tape. And I had just spoken to my mother, so I knew it could not be her.

'Hullo stranger,' she said, her voice carefully light.

'Colette,' I said. Even though it was three years since we'd last spoken, I knew straight away it was her.

'When did you get back?' she asked.

'About a month ago.'

'That's what I heard.'

I waited.

'How was Arizona?' she said.

'Brilliant.'

'I bet it was,' she said, her voice all grabby now. 'You deserved that.'

It was, I realised, as close to an apology as I was going to get.

'How's James?' I said, even though I knew they had split long before.

'James? God, that ended ages ago. Actually, you'll never guess. I'm engaged. To someone else, obviously.' She laughed.

'Congratulations.'

'Thanks, sweetie. Hey, you won't believe where I met him. Remember that awful coffee shop we used to go to in college?'

'No.'

'You do. Remember the time you got shortlisted for that essay award in first year? I stood on a table in there and announced it. Remember, I'd printed it up and started to read it out?'

I knew she brought that up to remind me there had been times she acted like a good friend. She probably hadn't met her fiancé there at all. But I could not help feeling pleased by the memory.

'You got us barred,' I said.

A hail of her laughter erupted, and relief seeped through me like sunlight.

'So, sweetie,' she said, 'my hen night is next month. I thought, a couple of nights in a villa in Tuscany, and the girls, lots of wine and tan topping up time. You'll come. Won't you?'

That evening, I walked across the city and into that small pub off Harcourt Street. After the traffic and the warm light of the setting sun, it was quiet and dark in there, smaller than I remembered. Behind the bar, a woman folded napkins. On the other side, a man sat on a stool, a half empty pint of Guinness beside the paper he was reading. I ordered a gin and tonic. Then I sat beside the empty fireplace, in the same place I had found James and Colette together, almost three years ago now, his hand resting casually on her thigh. I had left before either of them saw me, but the following morning, I called around to her. When she answered the door, she was wearing a red flannelette dressing grown, tied tightly around her.

'I just came to tell you,' I had said, 'that I never want to see you again.' And then I started the speech that had been simmering inside me all night. 'You are poison,' I said. 'All you do is hurt me.'

Her flatmate appeared in the hallway. Colette backed into it and I followed her, shutting the door hard behind us.

'Colette,' said her flatmate. 'Is everything okay?'

'All you do is hurt me,' I said again. I was crying by then, hotly, and my throat hurt and my head felt heavy. I forgot all the things I wanted to make her remember. My violin recital at school, when she laughed throughout in the wings. Our holiday in Goa, where she disappeared with some guy, leaving me alone for the whole second week. My graduation day when she faked an asthma attack and later confessed she'd done it because she had been bored.

Now, in her hallway, she watched me cry, her arms folded across her chest. Her flatmate had disappeared.

'He never loved you,' she said finally, her voice tinged with distaste. She shrugged. There had been nothing left to do but leave.

The villa was on the outskirts of a hilltop town that looked down onto the city of Florence. It had seven bedrooms, each high ceilinged and barely furnished. Colette said it was three hundred years old. Her dad had bought it two years earlier, with his second wife. They had since broken up and it was rarely used. There was a musty smell and one of the windows was broken. Weeds grew alongside the geraniums in the window boxes, and in the pots dotted along the steps to the pool. A vineyard met the fence that marked the edge of the garden. It was dusk when we arrived and below us, the city lights were like a reflection of the stars in the darkening sky.

That night, we sat on the loungers that surrounded the pool, drinking from the crates of wine bought from the neighbouring vineyard. Colette's friends were loud and cheerful. They talked about how strange it was to be in their thirties. They talked about ghosts and destiny and whether or not there might be a god. One girl said she dreamed she met God, and the next day she felt extraordinarily happy. Ever since then, she said, she knew, deep down, that the whole point was to strive to be the best person you could be.

'I wish I could believe in one,' I said. 'But it's hard, doing what I do.'

'Frances does medical research,' said Colette. 'She's an atheist. Tell them,' she said.

'It's sort of a new field,' I said. 'Using evolution theory to improve medicine. Like slowing antibiotic resistance in the body. Stuff like that.'

'How does that make you an atheist?' someone said.

'Well,' I said. 'There's no blueprint for the body, is there? It's just lots of different genes adapting so it can survive. That's why it makes mistakes when it's trying to get better from something. Like when you get diarrhoea to flush out a toxin, but then that can make you dehydrate and die.'

No one said anything. Around us, the cricket song seemed to grow louder.

'Tell them about diseases,' Colette said.

'Okay,' I said. 'Diseases. Some need the person to move about so they can spread. So you're sick and you don't even know it. And then ones like malaria need you to be so sick you can't even slap the mosquitoes anymore. So you feel sick. It's all genes fighting other genes to survive. Where's your God in all of that?'

'I guess he's doing a good job of hiding,' someone said.

'Bloody hell,' said someone else, 'way to take the kick out of being drunk.' We all laughed.

'Sorry,' I said. We opened more bottles of wine. We drank them. It must have been close to dawn when Colette and I wandered into the vineyard and picked some grapes. When we got back, the others had all gone to bed. We stood at the fence, staring down at the city.

'Like a magic carpet,' I said.

'Ah,' she said. 'That's what I missed.' She put her arm around my neck. She had to stand on tiptoe to do it. Then she kissed my cheek. 'My bestest friend,' she said. 'I'm so glad you're here.' And relief spilled over me again.

The next day, Colette's cough could be heard everywhere. The heavy dust in the villa had woken her asthma. I hadn't seen her have a proper attack since we were in college, but a girl called Lisa had. She told us, in front of a frowning Colette, how they'd called an ambulance in the end. Someone suggested we have another night around the pool instead of going out, just in case. But Colette said she was fine. She was not staying in on her hen night. What kind of girl did we take her for? In the early evening, three taxis came as planned, and wound us down through the hills, until we met the lights of the city, and entered them.

We were dropped at a cocktail bar recommended by Colette's dad, on the corner of a brightly lit square. The waiter showed us to a table on the terrace and we ordered our first round. When it came, Colette swigged from her drink and slapped her thigh and said damn. Later, she chatted with a group of American boys at the bar, even though it wasn't the kind of place you chatted to people at the bar. She was dressed to fasten eyes on her, in a fire engine red dress that gathered in flower shapes over her chest and ended with a fat satin border midway up her thigh. Her engagement ring caught and shone back the light. At one point, she looked at me and said,

'Honey, you didn't think of getting those old roots done before coming away with us girls?' She pouted. Someone tittered.

'No bitching allowed. That's the rule,' said someone.

'The rule,' said someone else, and everyone laughed this time. Everyone except Colette, who sniffed daintily before sipping her cocktail.

'I just thought if a girl was invited away on a weekend to glam it up with an old friend, she'd make a bit of an effort,' she said.

'Frances is a bookworm,' said the girl who had just spoken, who already looked and sounded drunk. 'They don't care what they look like. Frances, you look lovely,' she said then. 'You're a little angel.'

There was more tittering.

'I was just kidding, sweetie,' said Colette, smiling brightly. 'I know you don't have time for silly stuff like that with all your important work in the laboratory.'

I went to the bathroom, where I surveyed myself in the mirror. An inch of dull brown hair topped the rich red I had dyed it a couple of months earlier, just before I left Arizona. A crescent of mascara lay cradled beneath each eye. The skin on my nose was shiny. In the bright lighting, I could see how ill-suited my mustard top was to my pale skin. It was also too small for me; the long sleeves clung to my upper arms.

Lisa came in.

'That sounded worse than she meant it,' she said. 'You okay?'

'Sure,' I said, my voice shriller than I expected it to be.

When we got back, the Americans were sitting at our table. Colette was smoking a thin cigar and laughing loudly.

'Drink up, sweetie,' she said. 'You're falling behind.'

I took a large gulp. It was delicious – frothy and sweet with a hot, dark undercurrent of alcohol.

'Atta girl,' she said. Her skin glittered. Her eyes seemed to burn. 'Poor Frances doesn't get out much,' she said to the boy sitting beside her.

'That's a shame,' he said.

Then she turned her back to me. I finished my drink quickly and went to the bar to order another round, to have something to do.

One of the Americans followed.

'So how do you know the fabulous Colette?' he said. His voice sounded older than he looked.

'From school,' I said. 'She was a good place to hide behind.'

He laughed, his eyes lingering slightly longer than necessary on my face. He was so clean, so wealthy clean, with his short-sleeved shirt over a white t-shirt and glistening short hair and weighty-looking watch and the musky smell of aftershave.

When we got back from the bar, Colette was watching us. She ignored my smile.

'Back to the villa,' she said. 'Drink up, folks. Party time.'

In the taxi, his hand rested on my thigh. I looked out at the lights and leaned my back against his chest, his breath warm on my neck all the way to the villa where Stevie Wonder was already knocking out song after song from someone's phone and people were dancing around the pool. Lisa pulled me into her room, where she fixed my make-up, made me change into a dark blue dress.

'Look at you,' she said, and we looked at my reflection in the mirror.

The dress swooped in at my waist. It swung at my knees. It turned up the blue in my eyes.

'Who's a bookworm now?' she said. And we ran back out to the pool. But now, my American was nowhere to be seen. And there was no Colette. I sat on a lounger, talking to no one, anger drumming through me like pain. I kept my gaze on the flat surface of the water. When Lisa tried to pull me up to dance, I told her to leave me alone.

I was still sitting there when my American ran out of the house, bare-chested and frightened looking.

'She can't breathe,' he shouted.

We ran inside. Colette was lying on the bed, her mouth and eyes wide open. Each breath she took was a high-pitched wheeze that made you think of an injured animal. She reached an arm towards her bag on the ground and opened and closed her fist. She glared at us, then at her bag.

'Her inhaler,' said Teresa. And she emptied the bag. A mobile, lipstick and a notebook clattered against the ground.

'I'll check her bedroom,' I said.

'And someone call an ambulance,' she shouted.

It took over an hour for the ambulance to arrive.

'Her breathing's gone quiet,' someone said. 'Her lips have turned blue.'

Lisa went with her in the ambulance. The rest of us followed in taxis. The Americans had already left.

In intensive care, a doctor told us Colette was stable. She had suffered a minor brain injury from lack of oxygen. She would probably make a full recovery, he said, eventually, but they could not tell how long this would take. It could be months. It could be years.

As it has turned out, Colette hasn't fully recovered, at least not yet. It is one year on and she went back to work last week but to a new, less demanding position. She gets easily frustrated with herself, because she has lost her quickness. She can no longer demand the attention of everyone in a room, or reduce everyone around her to laughter. She is quiet. I know this because I visited her every second day for three months in the rehabilitation unit, and because now we meet up twice a week. She is very grateful to me for this. After a few months, things ended between her and her fiancé. We are two single ladies, and should be proud of it, I tell her. One of these days we will travel the world and leave this stupid country where it belongs – in its freezing, jellyfish-infested sea. She smiles when I say this, and her eyes grow wet and big.

Sometimes, when I wake in the night, or am travelling some-where by bus or by train, I see myself standing in the middle of that vineyard – that evening, after we'd returned from the hospital, and everyone else was in bed asleep. I see it very clearly; it is like looking at a film. The woman in it walks slowly and purposefully along an avenue of trees, warm light from a low sun filtering through the branches. She stops and takes the inhaler from her bag. She hunkers and places it beneath the leaf of a weed. Then she walks back to the villa and up the steps to the pool. Sitting on its edge, she lets herself fall in. Submerged in the water, she wraps her arms around her knees and pulls herself to the floor. A moment passes, and then she opens her body again and the water pushes her back to the surface. She looks at the red roofs of the city below her, and sucks in the summer sweetened air.

NONE OF US WILL BE OKAY

The petals came away with nothing but a tweak of protest. One day in that sun was enough to suck the life out of anything. He had found the rose on the bench encircling the magnolia tree in the centre of the courtyard. The only trace of the wedding party from the morning before, which they had watched from their bedroom window. A bride in a meringue dress kept shaking a sparkling shawl and returning it to her shoulders. Like a kid would. With her laughing bridesmaids and tensely-smiling groom, it had looked like a scene from a bad sitcom. Not to Claire of course. 'She looks happy,' had been her little contribution.

Leaning back so that the crown of his head met the rutted surface of the trunk, he took in the treacle branches criss-crossing the clean blue of the sky. The pink bleeding into cream flowers. From this angle they studded the view like huge butterflies pinned there for effect. She was going to drag him around again, have them join queues and lick ice creams. The fact it was their last day in the city made no difference. It would just be more of the same in the next place.

When her voice rang out his name, he loved her not. There she stood beneath the archway, in a skirt and a red t-shirt which, he knew though could not see, revealed most of her back. Not the dress then. Most likely not the first outfit tried on either. She had done something to her hair too, so that now it coiled around the nape of her neck like a sleeping snake. Before this holiday, he never noticed how vain she was.

'It doesn't look weird does it? Like I'm trying to look like your Princess Leela or something?'

'Leia. No it doesn't.'

Down the cobbled street they walked, towards the Duomo that waited with the sunlight.

'So what do you think?'

'About what?' He waited for the shrunk voice asking if he had not been listening.

'An outdoors day. Walking about. At the end, we can go to that wine bar.'

He forgot. She was doing the upbeat thing. Had been ever since they arrived.

'Okey-doke?' she said, tapping the top of his head with her rolled up map.

'Okey-doke.'

A gradual build-up of a series of errors. So said *Notes on Anatomy and Oncology*. The errors, it said, keep happening until one cell acts against its function. When this happens, the mutation transmits itself to neighbouring cells. The body, turning itself into a maze of collapsing dominos. Everywhere, tourists mowed through the network of thin streets and anorexic pavements. All the city wanted was for them to go home. Iron bars crossed the front of every window. Each door, massive, dark and studded with thick nails, was closed.

She didn't seem to notice anything that wasn't on her map. Now and then, she stopped and studied it and then on they would march, sometimes taking a left turn, sometimes a right. As though they had somewhere to be an hour ago. Once, at a market, watching her try to choose between two leather bags, he felt sorry for her. She had not tried to hold his hand today. Yesterday he complained of the heat and she had taken hers back without comment.

'I'll wait over there,' he said, pointing to the steps leading to a large church the colour of rust. Trading shade for space. The sun burned his face and sandalled feet. A drop of sweat trickled down his chest. Wiping the back of his hand across his forehead he found a layer there too. His body regulating its temperature. The first night he saw Sam with the sweats, he thought he had just taken a shower in his jocks and t-shirt. No one could tell him how or why the cancer caused them. Not a single book or article addressed it. It was a symptom, they said, and that was all.

That was the first night he stayed home, sending the parents out for dinner. Before Sam fell asleep, they passed the time by taking photographs of each of their younger sister's twenty-four pairs of shoes and then posting them, along with her mobile number, on a website for the free exchange of things no longer wanted by their owners. They laughed for so long, you would think they had been stoned. When they finally stopped, Sam said – the first and only time he said anything like it to him –

'I'll shake this thing, won't I, Dave?'

Shake it. As though it were a nasty cold.

'Jesus. Of course you will.'

He hadn't noticed her walk up the steps. Standing before him, her silhouette hid the sun and it hid her. All he could see was the bottle of sun factor she held out, a glimmer from her sunglasses.

'You'll burn up sitting here,' she said.

The Bobili gardens, it turned out, were built on an incline. Another crowd versus pain dilemma. Apparently, this one was not his to solve. One avenue after the other, Claire walked, never pausing to enjoy the shade from the looming Cypress trees on each side.

Close to the top, he sat on a bench. For a while he occupied himself by ripping a large leaf into small shreds. Unusually, the edgy tang of sweat reached him from the other edge of the bench where she came and sat, her mouth pursed shut and her eyebrows scrunched over her closed eyes. Apparently she had given up her role as relationship conversationalist. He was not convinced she would not start crying. The idea had words running out of him.

'You know plants can get cancer?' he said.

Her eyes opened. 'I didn't know that.'

'Makes sense when you think about it, it's all about evolution anyway.'

Another quick glance to check she was listening.

'It's why it spreads. One cell mutates. That one's more likely to survive than the others. Then they all start copying it.'

'Oh.'

By the time they had taken their seats by the window of the small bar, a glass of white for her, red for him, it looked like Claire's efforts to exhaust herself had only been partially successful. All of her face except her eyes looked tired.

'This is nice,' she whispered into her glass. When he said nothing she said,

'Isn't it?'

'Yeah. Great.'

'Have you enjoyed yourself?' He wasn't imagining the sarcasm. He would dive in. It didn't matter.

'Not really. Have you?'

No lip quiver, nothing. She just looked out the window at the people walking home. Would they fly back early? Together? Would she go on alone? The questions flew at him like disturbed flies. He looked into the still red surface of his wine. The day they first turned up at the clinic, he was in what his mother called one of his moods. Who takes a morning off work because their little brother has the mumps? Little brother of 21 years after all, who is more than capable of taking himself. Then they found out about his white blood cell count. Nineteen thousand per micro-litre of blood. More than twice that of a normal count. Sam's body, no longer giving a shit about Sam. Starting to get everything screwy. No, that was wrong. Sam's body never gave a shit about him.

'I just don't get your fascination with all these places. Like yesterday. Why did we spend an hour looking at the plates some dead prince slobbered over?'

Rule number one of breaking up with somebody – always let them do the ranting. A slit of dark between her lips as she stared back at him, wide-eyed. A fleck of wetness on her cheek that must have come from him. Then she said it.

'Sam got better, David.'

The blur of people in departures presented itself. 'We don't say better.' He was standing now. 'Not until five years, remember?'

'They said he was okay.'

Everyone else was going in the opposite direction. He didn't let that slow him down, not even when some of them threw angry Italian words after him. He kept walking until he got to a large, tourist-ridden square. By now, the sun was about to disappear behind the buildings on the west side and half the square was the colour of warm gold, the other half in shadow. He phoned him there, right in the centre, where the crowd seemed to thin a little.

'Well. How's the man?' His voice crackled.

'Dave? Are you at the circus or something?'

'What's going on?'

'Not much. Played footie yesterday. Just five a side on the green with the lads.'

He got to the edge, sat down in the shade of a loggia that ran along one side of the square. At the other end, a violinist was playing a fast classical piece, her body moving with the music. He kept his gaze on her because he had to keep it on something.

'I've known him as long as I've known you, you know. That's three years in case you'd forgotten.'

The rims of Claire's eyes matched the colour of her t-shirt. As she spoke, the music stopped. A burst of applause clattered from the fat doughnut of tourists gathered around the violin player.

'And I know what this feels like.'

'You just said he got better.' He was facing her again, ready to throw back this new attack. Her cute little heart-shaped face was all crumpled.

'I'm not talking about Meg. Not exactly.'

Her sister had died in a car accident when Claire was thirteen years old, ten years before they met. Since Sam's diagnosis, he hated her for it. The realisation turned something down. He felt his shoulders slacken. A well-adjusted girl, his father had once said of her. He knew what he meant. She never let anything phase her. Always happy to go with the flow. Always the first to shrug off something not going to plan. On occasion in the past, it had irked him. Left him wondering how deep her feelings went for him. Went for anything.

Now, for the first time, he understood.

'I need to know he'll be okay.'

'He got through this.'

This time he took her hand, laced their warm fingers.

Later that evening they sat on the balcony of their hotel bedroom, wrapped in bathrobes and finally ready for sleep. In the courtyard below, the magnolias signalled up to them like unlit candles.

Long after they had sunk into darkness and she was in bed asleep, he returned to the window. Just the day before, Sam played football on the green again. That crazy beanpole body jostled against others, threw shouts out of it when called for, weaved around the ball, danced in and out of the long shadows of the trees thrown across the grass by the late afternoon sun. For now, working in his favour. For now, letting him be.

This new happiness was like falling.

HELEN

'Helen,' said Teresa again. 'Did you hear what I said?'

'You're going to visit Sarah in Italy.' The drum of her washing machine had started building speed.

'That's right,' she said. 'And the other thing is, I'd like you to come with me. Helen, is your TV broken or something?'

I looked up at her then.

'You haven't taken your eyes off that thing since you got here.'

'You'll hardly want me out there with you,' I said.

'I'll *need* you out there.'

The drum started spinning louder, the table was slightly vibrating. I could feel it in my hand when I placed it palm down on the surface.

'For God's sake,' she said. 'Who says no to a free trip to Europe?'

'Me?'

'Helen,' she said. 'I can't go without you.'

I knew it was true. As pleased as she was about Sarah being back in touch after all those years, you could tell part of her was also terrified at the idea of being on her own with her daughter. In a foreign country too.

'Well, she'd hardly want to see me,' I said.

'You're my best friend, of course she'd want to see you. It's on me. The flights anyway. I've been saving half my tips ever since she asked me.'

'How long ago was that?'

'A few months.'

I didn't say anything.

'Look, it's not like we'd be staying with her or anything. She's found us a nice little reasonable hotel.'

'Ah.'

'What does that mean?'

'Nothing.'

'Frank can't object,' she said then. It was a statement and a question at the same time. 'I mean, you guys aren't together anymore.'

It was a month since Frank and I had decided to take another temporary break. This was the first time she'd brought him up since I'd told her.

She looked at me hard and closely.

'If I haven't asked you much about him,' she said, 'maybe it's because I think it's a good thing.'

'Okay.'

'You're not back together?'

'Nope.'

'Good,' she said. 'Because he didn't make you happy.'

I drained my coffee. 'You know,' I said, looking around the room. 'It was in this kitchen I first met Sarah.'

She looked around the room too. 'It was?'

'One night I brought you home. Must have been a work night out. This was back when you still worked in Global. She was sitting right at this table with her schoolbooks out. In the middle of the night.'

Teresa stared at the table, as though if she looked at it hard enough, she'd remember.

'She didn't even say hello or ask what had happened or anything. Just told me to put you on the couch.'

'She's come a long way,' she said eventually.

'She's gone a long way too!'

Teresa looked at me.

'I mean, I thought that when she got the Princeton scholarship. But now Italy!'

'Now Italy.'

'Only now,' I said, 'are you guys are back in touch.'

'Distance makes the heart grow fonder,' said Teresa.

'Maybe.'

'Why are you being mean?'

'I'm sorry,' I said. Because she was right, I was being mean.

'Well, what do you say?' she said. 'Will you come with me or not?'

Maybe what I knew wasn't that she wouldn't go without me, but that she wouldn't go without the *idea* of me going with her, at least right up to when it was time to leave. If I was to not show up in the airport – a sudden dose of Covid or something – she probably would get on the plane without me.

Another thing had occurred to me too.

'Alright then,' I said. 'Why not?'

'Really? You're coming?'

'If you insist.'

'Yay!' she said, coming over and trying to wrap her arms around me.

'Alright, alright.'

The washing machine had stopped spinning. Now the clothes were lying still in the bottom half of the window.

'Are you okay?' she said.

'I'm fine.'

'The woman who's always fine.'

When I opened the door to Frank, he was wearing a freshly ironed shirt under his jacket and he smelled of aftershave; I wouldn't have been surprised if he'd produced a bouquet of flowers. Down the hall he followed me like a visitor. Or like someone I had just started seeing. Not the person who'd spent most of the past four years living in that apartment with me.

'You're looking well,' I said, when we reached the living room.

'You too,' he said. He grinned again.

'Thanks.' I'd managed to get out of work a few minutes earlier than I was supposed to, to grab a quick shower and do my hair the way he once said suited me.

'Do you want a beer?' I asked.

'A beer?'

The text I'd sent the day before had asked if he wanted to come round for a coffee.

'Okay, sure,' he said.

I waited until he had awkwardly settled himself in the armchair. It was weird seeing him there, still in his jacket. Like someone else's boyfriend.

'You cold or something?' I said.

'Cold?'

'Why don't you take off your jacket?'

He looked down at himself, like he hadn't known he was wearing one. Then he shrugged. 'I'm good,' he said.

'Suit yourself.' I took the beers out of the fridge. 'So. How've you been?'

'Good. Yeah. You?'

'Great.'

I handed him a beer and sat on the sofa, close enough so we could clink.

'I just thought,' I said, 'it was maybe time to check in?'

'Totally.'

'It's been like a month.'

He shook his head. Then he looked at the brochures I'd arranged on the coffee table, the top one with the Duomo and colosseum in Rome and the leaning tower of Pisa all beside each other, as though in real life they stood together on the same street.

'What's all this?' he said. I knew by the way he said it that he'd been scrolling my Facebook.

'Oh. Teresa dropped those in earlier,' I said. 'She's doing this big trip to Italy to see Sarah. Asked me to come along.'

His eyes widened, pretending surprise. He definitely already knew about it. Even if he hadn't seen my posts, someone would have told him.

'Wow,' he said. 'Sounds good.'

'You think?'

He gulped his beer. 'You could do with a vacation.'

I didn't say anything to that.

'Won't be cheap,' he grimaced.

'Teresa says she's paying. For the flights anyway.'

'The waitress is paying?' He was genuinely amused. 'While the newly appointed manager goes free?'

'It's her big idea. I don't even know if I want to go.'

'I'm only kidding. What part of Italy?'

'Florence,' I said.

'Oh yeah. Sarah got some other kind of scholarship out there, didn't she? For something.'

'A master's in art history. Whatever that means.'

'Florence, Italy. What would you and Teresa do in a place like that?'

He was really wondering.

'Apparently there's an itinerary.'

'Well. A free trip to Europe. You'd be crazy not to go.'

'So everyone keeps telling me.'

'Nice they've made up after everything.'

'It's very forgiving,' I said, 'of Sarah.'

'No, totally,' he said. 'Totally.' He shook his head. 'Didn't Teresa once go on a bender for a whole week? Left Sarah home alone?'

This was a story I had once told him.

'What age was she, ten?'

'Twelve.'

'Still.' He shook his head. The beer bottle shot to his lips again. 'I suppose Teresa does have her act together these days. When are you flying out?'

Then, before I had even answered, he stood. He put one hand on the back of the armchair he'd been sitting on, and looked around the room, like he forgot something and couldn't remember what it was.

That's when I understood. That the aftershave wasn't for my sake. Or the ironed shirt under the jacket.

I didn't want to say anything. But if I didn't, he would leave anyway.

'You're not seeing someone else,' I said.

And at first, it seemed that it was okay, that what I said was true – he looked at me like he couldn't understand what he was hearing, as though he'd never even contemplated such a thing.

But then his face just sort of dropped into the way it wanted to look. The way he felt.

Tired.

A kid back in front of the school principal and not giving a damn anymore.

'Oh my God,' I said. Without really registering what I was doing, I went to the sink and poured myself a glass of water. I put it on the counter.

It felt like the air was being sucked out of me.

'Helen,' he said, in a useless kind of way.

'How long.'

'Not long.'

And then she came to me. The new girl at his Christmas party. I could see her as though she was standing back in front of me all dark-haired and stupidly pouty.

I had known all along, ever since then, even though at the same time I hadn't.

'That girl,' I said, 'with the zip dress.'

He didn't say anything.

'You've been cheating on me,' I said. 'Since fucking Christmas.'

'No,' he said. 'It only started last month. Just before we split up.'

'It was my understanding we didn't split up,' I said. 'We took a *break*. Like the last time.'

'It's the same thing.'

The same thing.

'No it isn't.' I thought I might start crying then but I didn't. 'What about us?' I said.

'Helen, come on.'

'Come on what?'

'There is no us.'

'What's that supposed to mean?'

'It means,' he said, and I saw with alarm that he was building up some courage. 'It means that the only reason we were ever together in the first place was because we got along okay and we both wanted children and time was running out.'

'This is not happening.' Because what he said wasn't true, it wasn't true at all. I remembered distinctly liking him when I met him at that party. It wasn't long after I moved to Lexington. I remembered liking lots about him. One thing was that even though he'd known Teresa longer than I did, he seemed a bit intimidated by her. That had been nice. And then, when I told him I'd moved to Lexington to be closer to my sister, and ended up mentioning how she and her family now live in Chicago, he didn't make a big thing out of it. That was nice as well. Most people either made out it was some kind of tragedy or just looked at me like I'd said something that didn't add up. If I didn't exactly find him the most attractive man I'd ever met, it hadn't seemed like I wasn't attracted to him either. He'd kept smiling at me in a twinkly-eyed sort of way.

It was then, that first time we met, that it had dawned on me – maybe *this* was everyone else's secret. Maybe this is what it feels like when you meet The One. Comfortable. And *not* the way it had been that one time, a million years ago. As if that feeling could last more than five minutes.

'Look,' he said. 'I know it's been tough. But we didn't even try very hard.'

'*You* didn't try very hard,' I said. I couldn't look at him now.

'And I remember you once saying you were never one of those women who always dreamed of having kids.'

'I never said that.'

'Yes you did.'

'Well, even if I did, what has that to do with anything?'

'Well, just that maybe it wasn't *meant* to happen for us. Maybe we were never meant to have kids. Together I mean. And at least now, we're free.'

'This is what you say,' I said, 'after doing four whole years with someone'.

'You make it sound like a prison sentence.'

'Fuck you.'

'Someday, you'll meet someone too,' he said. 'Then you'll see I was right.'

And just like that, he turned away, walked out the door and closed it behind him. His footsteps made fast work of the stairs to the entrance below. And the next day, when I came back from work all his things were gone. Clothes, workout stuff, everything. The only thing he left was the watch I got him for Christmas.

By the time we were on the train in the darkening dusk to the city of Florence, frightened-looking poppies flashing along the track, we had all the polite stuff out of the way, and I found myself unable to say much to either of them. Even when Italy Sarah, who in a white shirt and sunglasses was more like someone from the television than the awkward teenager I remembered, asked about my promotion and if I still lived in the same apartment. Even when the man who came round to check our tickets told me off in Italian for putting my feet on the seat opposite mine, and then sighed loudly when I couldn't find my ticket straight away. Even when we walked those nasty little streets to the hotel. The only time I piped up was when we were standing there in that tiny lobby while Sarah marked 'some nice restaurants' as she put it on a map for us.

The McDonald's was just like the ones at home. If people had been speaking English, it would have been hard to tell the difference.

'I wish everyone would stop talking,' I said, when we had gotten our food and found a table. 'It gives me the creeps when I don't know what they're saying.'

Teresa, who'd made such a show of being mortified when I had asked Sarah for directions there was already attacking her Big Mac as though she may never eat again.

'I suppose we'll get used to it,' she said, a smidge of ketchup on her upper lip. Then she reached out and pressed my hand. 'Can you believe it,' she said, more or less when she'd swallowed her mouthful.

'Believe what.'

She smiled. 'I don't know. That we're here. How beautiful Jane is.'

She waited for me to say something.

'Did you see how fluently she spoke to the receptionist in the hotel?' she continued.

'It was impressive,' I said.

'Wasn't it?'

'It must feel weird though.'

'Weird?'

'To see her all grown up. After all these years.'

She thought about it. 'I'm in awe of her,' she said.

'Sure,' I said. Then I said, 'I guess it makes sense.'

She looked at me. Tired and maybe a tad wary.

'I just mean, I guess she liked the idea of turning into somebody new. After everything.'

'That's true,' she said. 'That's true.'

'I wouldn't worry about her having to leave so quickly,' I said.

'She's booked pretty much the whole week off to spend with me. I mean, us.'

'Are we meeting the fiance?'

'I think so.'

'When?'

'I don't know.'

'What about his parents? They live here too, don't they?'

'Sarah didn't say anything.'

'Oh,' I said. 'I see.'

'I think I need a nap,' she said. She laughed unconvincingly. 'We're both tired.'

'No way are you dragging me across the Atlantic ocean for a nap,' I said. 'Hey, did you notice that place we passed on our way here? A cocktail bar, I think? It was on a square.'

She frowned, as though she couldn't recall the place. Of course she could recall it.

'It's fine,' I said. 'I understand. The last thing you want to do now you're here is to start drinking again. Right?'

'Right.'

'Unless – you want to try a virgin?' I made a please face. I pressed my hands together as though in prayer. 'I can't remember the last time I was on vacation,' I said. 'I can't remember the last time I had a strawberry daiquiri.'

We got a table out on the terrace, beside a big raucous group of girls. When our drinks came, I lifted mine and held it there until she lifted hers and we clinked.

'To having fun,' I said.

'To having fun,' she said.

We each took a sip from our straws.

'Wow, that's good,' I said. 'How's your virgin?'

'Delicious.'

The waiter came out again with a tray loaded with pale pink drinks in martini glasses. He placed them on the table where the girls were sitting.

'Round three,' said one, in an English accent. 'How many cocktails do you make?'

'Fifty-two,' he said. 'We serve fifty-two cocktails at Il Maestro.' When they all laughed at this, I laughed along. I smiled at Teresa. But she turned her gaze out at the square and squinted. She put on her sunglasses. She sat like that the whole time, every now and then turning to take a big sip.

I took my time finishing my drink.

'I'm just going to order one more,' I said, when it was finally gone. 'If you don't mind. Those pink ones looked amazing.'

Walking back to the hotel, we did not say one word to each other. In the lobby, she said she thought she'd have an early night and I didn't see her again until breakfast the following morning, when we were back to polite conversation, like a pair of strangers. And that was the way it stayed, all week the bad feeling hardening between us like concrete.

If Sarah noticed, she didn't say. Every day she brought us somewhere worse. The first morning, it was the Duomo, fat and stuck in its cramped little square. It took one hundred and fifty years to build,

Sarah said. It was six hundred years old. Inside, all dull marble and gloom, she told us about a man who was killed in there, hundreds of years ago, how they'd stabbed him nineteen times because some family wanted to take power from another family, and how the other family had retaliated by killing other people and hanging their bodies from a window. Then she had us climb the bell tower beside it, all four hundred and fourteen steps, dark and with an ancient smell of cold, the steps getting narrower and narrower towards the top, the view when we got up there nothing but rooftops all the way to the horizon, like the whole city was stuck in a globe. The day after that, she took us to an old bridge over a dirty looking river. There were jewellery shops squeezed together all along the bridge. It looked like the whole thing might one day collapse into the river. Then the man explained that once, it *had* collapsed into it. Back then it used to be all butcher shops up there. They would slaughter the trapped animals right there on the bridge and throw their foul-smelling meat waste into the river below. One minute the butchers were selling their meat and people were buying it from them, weighing it up and seeing how far their money would stretch, and another they were all falling and then drowning and then gone. The next day we queued for two hours to see the statue of David. While we were waiting, Sarah explained how he had learned the human body by painting corpses in a hospital. That once he had to hide himself for two whole months in someone's basement because of a death threat out on him. Then it was a palace all yellow stone and small windows, where inside the walls were covered with pictures of battle scenes, people being slaughtered from hundreds of years ago. Afterwards, a big market, where they sold shoes and sunglasses and chickens and rabbits, skinned but still in one piece, lined up in neat little rows.

At least, all that was left for me to survive was dinner in a restaurant that evening with Sarah and her fiancé and his parents, and one last full day. After that we would be flying back home.

'These are nice,' said Teresa, lifting a scarf from a little stall I'd stopped at, selling knitted things. 'Isn't all this a bit like the stuff you used to do?'

That day, she and Sarah were trying extra hard to be nice to me.

'A little, I guess.'

'Helen used to knit stuff,' she said to Sarah. 'She had a market-place on Etsy.'

'You did? Wow, like a proper business? That's really cool.'

'Crotchet. It wasn't a proper business.' I'd never been able to figure out the marketing, and there'd been so many other people selling afghans and tea towels with a button hook. Still, looking at the things on that stall, it came back to me as though it was yesterday I was in that place I used to buy my yarn. I must have spent hours there choosing the shades. Then coming up with the patterns. All the trialling and erroring that followed, until something came out right.

'Well, I bet it was amazing. Why'd you stop?' said Sarah.

'Why'd I stop? I mean, it was just a thing I did. Before my mother died.'

'Oh.'

'Then I moved and got the job in Global. You know, the call centre? Where I met your mother?'

'Right.'

'You were still doing it when you moved to Lexington,' said Teresa.

'I don't think so.'

'You were. I remember you talking about it.'

'That's good, isn't it? A memory from those days.'

'These are sweet,' said Sarah. She was holding up a blue baby cardigan.

Up to then I hadn't noticed them.

'Well, I bet it was wonderful, Helen,' she said, putting the cardigan back down.

'You do?' I said. 'Why?' I laughed, to show I wasn't annoyed.

She shook her head, did a quizzical face. Still smiling. She glanced at Teresa, who was not smiling.

'Why what?' said Jane.

'Why do you bet it was wonderful? I mean, do you mean you bet the pieces I crotcheted were wonderful, or that I had a wonderful time crotcheting, or that I was wonderful to do it?'

She looked at Teresa. Teresa rolled her eyes.

'Well. I don't know,' said Sarah.

Teresa was staring at me but I didn't look back at her.

'It's no big deal,' I said. 'I guess we aren't all destined to live a charmed life.'

'I'm sorry,' began Sarah.

'How's your headache?' said Teresa.

Earlier, when we were finished in the palace and Sarah suggested we go to another church, I mentioned I had a headache so we went to look for a pharmacy instead.

'Still bad,' I said.

'Maybe you should go back to the hotel and lie down,' she said.

'Maybe I will.'

'No problem,' said Teresa. 'And don't feel like you have to come this evening either if you don't feel up to it.'

That evening, back in McDonald's, I tried to imagine what it would be like back home without Frank or Teresa. But all I could think of was work, and even then I wasn't actually thinking about work itself, but its long blue and grey room, row after row of people selling. Back in the cocktail place, which didn't feel the same, maybe because it was so busy and I was the only person there alone, I had four cocktails in a row. For all I knew, I was going to be around for another forty-two years. Or maybe I only had one left. What difference did it make, either way? Whether or not a person has friends, or whether or not her sister wants her in her life. Sooner or later we would all be gone, like the people in the battle scenes. Like the man in the church. That was the only thing anyone could be sure of, so it was the only thing that mattered.

The following morning, after breakfasting alone, I found Teresa and Sarah in the lobby.

'Here she is,' said Sarah. The two of them smiling at me.

'How's the headache?' said Teresa.

As usual, I'd woken hours before I needed to, but this time with a sharp, real headache, which so far the paracetamol hadn't touched.

'Fine,' I said.

'Great,' said Sarah.

Now was the time for me to apologise, if I was going to.

'How was dinner?' I said.

'Lovely,' said Teresa. 'Thanks.'

'Glad to hear it,' I said.

'Well, that's good you're feeling better,' said Sarah. 'So today, we're going to the Uffizi. It's basically one of the best art galleries in the world. I've booked the tickets already so we won't even have to queue.' Looking at me with this last bit.

'Sounds great, darling,' said Teresa.

There was a moment then, when, if I said I hadn't slept well, and that they should go on without me, it would have been fine. If anything, they would only have been relieved. But I couldn't do it. It felt impossible. As though, if I did, I would be drawing some vast attention upon myself, and then only to be alone again, but still somehow in that vast attention. Everything was impossible except to follow them, one step after another all the way back along those streets. It was the same when we were inside that terrible dark and neverending place, long heavy rooms full of old religious paintings that seemed to drain the last bit of energy I had into themselves. Like a child, I followed them, always keeping at a safe distance. Every time they stopped to look at a painting, I pretended to be looking at another one nearby. That's how I came to see the one with the angel.

In one way, it was just like all the others – the virgin Mary and the baby Jesus. But in this one, two baby angels are for some reason holding up Jesus. One is gazing at him, but the other one is look-ing right out the painting and he is smiling. As though the two big weird orange, heavy-looking wings jutting out of his back aren't a problem. As though they aren't even there. Mary, though she looks so mournful, isn't looking at Jesus either, even though he is looking at her, sadly. She is looking at the angel, as though almost diverted by him. The angel's hand is on Jesus' knee. On his shoulder, a chubby foot rests heavily, in that selfish baby way, toes splayed, the big one grazing the angel's hand.

The way he is looking around, it's like someone has called his name, and he's still smiling from his game.

Filippo Lippi, the little notice beside it read. 1406–1469. His wife, it said, was his model for Mary. The angel may have been based on his son.

His mother, telling him dinner is ready.

The security guard must have been watching me the whole time because suddenly there he was, standing beside me and all but yelling at me. Even though he spoke in Italian, I knew what he was saying. Look what you've done. Putting your hand like that on a priceless painting. What were you thinking? That is not the way one ought to behave. Like the ticket inspector on the train. Teresa and Sarah were by him now, staring, as were other people who happened to be around.

'You touched it?' said Sarah.

'Why?' said Teresa.

I tried to answer. But what was there to say? That for a moment, I had believed that the angel was my baby? I had never had a baby. My single solitary pregnancy hadn't even lasted the first trimester. When the doctor in the hospital finally relented and did the ultrasound, it had been just as she'd said. All you could see was the swirling of blood and tissue.

It felt like I was running forever and because I was running, room after room, people kept turning to look at me. Even outside, as I kept running, past a fake statue of David and another statue of a man holding another man's head, veins and sinews dangling out of it, and back to the streets, people kept staring. Does no one ever run in Florence I wanted to ask them? Is it against a law or something? I wanted to shout it. Maybe I was going to when I tripped, on an uneven flagstone I think, yanking me hard down onto the pavement, so that I grazed my knees like a child. I cried like a child as well, bunched against a wall. Except to say it like that doesn't get it right. It was more like – the crying started happening to me. It was a thing happening in my body and I just had to let it. The sounds coming out of me, the ache, the wetness, it was all just happening, until it stopped and someone was tapping my knee. I opened my eyes to see a policeman, hunkered down beside me. I don't know how long he'd been there. Youngish, in his uniform. He had a serious moustache.

'Okay?' he said. He looked like he really hoped I was okay.

'Okay,' I said.

That was when, beyond him, Teresa appeared, on the far end of that street. This way and that she looked, her face tight with worry. My first thought was that Sarah, finally tired of me, had left, and she was looking for her. Then Sarah joined her and I saw that, despite everything, it was me she was looking for. All that worry was on my account. In that moment, the threads I knew of her difficult life shone and shame washed over me, as she looked back the way she'd come, scanned again the moving crowd, before her gaze swung back to the street where I sat waiting.

Just before setting eyes on me, she called my name.

THE EDGE OF
HAPPINESS

That was a beautiful summer.

In the mornings, she worked on the nursery. Walls she painted Sunlight Yellow. Curtains she fashioned out of a lovely soft cotton, cream with small red flowers, which she had bought years before and never used; when hung, they shirked against the open windows, before swelling with the breeze. When the wooden crib arrived, she painted it Fire Engine Red and placed it in the centre of the room. Hung above it a mobile of fat, furry bees.

In the afternoons, she walked the hill behind the house, and took in the network of fields, dotted here and there by houses and the odd copse of trees, crows flying their straight black lines across the sky, swallows drawing their more elaborate messages. She lay on the grass, and talked to the baby growing inside her.

In the evenings, she and Thomas ate together, out on the terrace. She prepared simple, delicious meals, like grilled trout with baked sweet potato, or chicken Provençale, salty with anchovies and olives.

'You really do seem happy here,' he said one evening, after they'd eaten and were still sitting outside.

'Told you.'

'I'm glad.'

'It feels –' She paused. 'Now, don't laugh.'

He gave a faux-solemn nod.

'It feels like –'

He was looking at her. He was listening.

'A state,' she continued in a lilting voice to show she knew how silly she sounded, 'of grace.'

'Hm.'

'I know.' She laughed at herself.

A quick gesture with his eyes and she scraped her seat towards him, draped her legs across his lap.

'Ever since we moved here though,' she continued, speaking into his shoulder, 'it's like I'm humming with it. All day when you're at work, and I hardly talk to anyone, it feels like everything happens perfectly, just when it's supposed to. And I'm floating along.'

'Hormones?'

'Hormones! Maybe hormones. Whatever that means.'

'Ever felt like this before?'

'Maybe.' She thought about it. 'In Italy, maybe. There was a morning in Florence. You wanted to see those Dali sketches of Dante's inferno.'

'You sat on that square for nearly three hours on your own. Reading.'

'And drinking those tiny cappuccinos. One after the other.'

'We won't be having holidays like that again for a while.'

'I suppose not.'

He put his hand on her stomach, which had been swelling for over seven months.

'Still on Daniel, if it's a boy?' she said.

'Yes, Daniel.'

'Polly for a girl.'

'Polly.'

He moved his hand back and forth slowly. Kissed the top of her head again. It was a Friday night and they had no plans that weekend. The kiss started hard and stayed that way. They had barely reached the bedroom before most of their clothes were lying on different parts of the floor.

Two months later, a baby boy was born, right on time. It was a natural birth. Everything went as it should have done. More or less anyway, only a few stitches were needed. She barely felt them after the painkillers wore off. She was too busy being in thrall to Daniel, new perfect Daniel who slept so beautifully – in his hospital cot or on her chest or in Thomas' arms – and who could latch on straight away like a pro when she tried to breastfeed him. She barely slept at all those two days and then when she got back home, there were visitors – her mother and Thomas' parents, who wanted to help but who she really did not need. They all kept saying how tired she must be, but she didn't feel tired at all. Really, she just wanted them all to leave. She wanted to get on with her new life as a mother. Establish its new routines, learn its new corners. If only she could sleep, Thomas said, but really she no longer seemed to need to. It was as though in giving birth she had somehow attained a superpower, which meant she would never feel tiredness again.

The fear began when a nurse who came to weigh Daniel said his weight gain was a bit slow. But he was a good feeder, the nurse had said, his latch was good. She was sure his weight would come on soon. For now, it was just something to keep an eye on. But this didn't reassure Jane at all. That day, she got Thomas to go out and buy some formula, which she started feeding Daniel alongside all the breastfeeding. She bought fenugreek tablets online, which she read could increase her milk supply. Whenever he was awake and not feeding (and that was rare, even after she started giving him formula as well), she would try to coax him to latch on, because she had also read that the more he fed, the greater her supply would be. She didn't care how raw and sore her nipples had become, or even that they sometimes bled. She barely noticed it. She bought an electric pump, and took to pumping her breasts when he was asleep, to stimulate further milk supply. But nothing seemed to work. At least, nothing assuaged her fear that he was not thriving, even after the nurse came back and said his weight gain had improved. It was the way Daniel would writhe and cry while trying to feed from her. Like it was hopeless and he wasn't getting anything at all. The nurse said that rest was the thing she needed. Thomas said the same thing, that she just needed to sleep. But not once did she feel like sleeping. Sleep for Jane belonged to a different, parallel world. Not the world she was in. When she wasn't feeding or pumping or soothing or nappy changing, she would do housework. It was important Daniel was not exposed to any germs, especially if he had not gained enough weight. He wouldn't be as able to fight an infection as another baby might. Thomas said she was overdoing it, that he could do all the housework. That that's what he was doing already. But he was not keeping it as clean as it needed to be. Anyone could see that. She ignored him.

Sometimes, at night, in the bursts of time when Daniel slept, she would walk through the rooms of the house at night trying to see if there was anything she missed. After that, if Daniel was still asleep, she might wander out into the garden, coming back inside to sit down on the couch only when the pain from the stitched-up wound inside her became too much. If Daniel was still asleep then, she would take him out of his cot anyway, and feed him on the couch. Sometimes then it would feel like she was watching the scene, rather than being in it. That there was Jane and Daniel, on the couch, and then there was she, outside and looking in, feeling nothing.

One morning, her husband walked in to find her sitting there, and for a moment she did not recognise this tall, broad man. It lasted only a moment. When it passed, she told him about the caterpillars eating the herbs in the garden. There were hundreds of them, she said. Then she told him how the man next door had left his porch light on all night. How he had left it on every night that week and how, only yesterday, she had seen him looking strangely at her when she was in the front garden.

Thomas stared at her. 'Have you been up all night?'

'Not all night,' she said.

'You need to rest,' he said.

'I'm fine,' she told him. 'I'm not even tired.'

'I could ring work,' he said doubtfully. 'Take an extra leave day?' It was his first day back at work. Two weeks after Daniel had been born.

'Don't be ridiculous. Why would you do that?'

By the time he got home that evening, the house was as clean as usual, dinner was ready, and Daniel was sleeping peacefully in the Moses basket. And somehow Jane knew that, somewhere in the house, a camera had been installed. She had felt it on her all day. Now, by the way he was looking at her, she knew it was Thomas who had put it there.

'Jesus,' he said. He was really staring at her. At her body.

She looked down and noticed the small stain on her dress.

'Is it – normal?' he asked. 'At this stage, I mean.'

'What do you mean?'

'It looks like a lot. Of blood, I mean.'

'It's the stitches,' she said. 'I think something's happened to them.' She had realised she was hurting.

'Jesus,' said Thomas. 'How did you not notice?'

She shook her head.

'We're going to the hospital. The last thing you want is an infection.'

On the way, he pulled into a petrol station.

'It's nearly empty.' He turned to her. 'You want anything? Water?'

'No.'

'I'll get water. Two seconds, okay?'

As soon as he was inside the petrol station, she got out of the car. She opened the back seat, took out Daniel, who was asleep. Then she knocked on the passenger seat window of the car in front of theirs. A teenage boy was sitting there.

'Get out of the car,' she said.

The teenager looked alarmed but he didn't do anything.

'Get out,' she said. 'I need this car. It's an emergency.' She opened his door.

'Mum,' shouted the boy, trying to close the door. He was strong. 'Mum.' And then he put his hand on the horn and kept it there.

'This child is in danger,' she shouted over the din. 'Just get out.'

But then Thomas was coming out of the station. He was running towards her.

A narrow path bordered the road. She reached it and kept walking.

'You keep away,' she shouted back at Thomas.

A lorry roared past. It blared its horn, a warning to her. She held Daniel tight against her chest. He was awake now, and nuzzling into her, already trying to latch on, to feed.

'Jane.' Her husband was beside her, his arm on her shoulder. 'Where the hell do you think you're going?'

She shook his hand off but he put it back.

'Get away from me,' she told him. 'I know about the camera.' She flashed him a look. 'You won't take him away from me.'

A car passed. She put out her hand. She would hitch to the nearest city. She had her credit cards.

'Call an ambulance,' Thomas shouted back towards the station. 'Jane, I don't know what to do. Please. Give me Daniel.'

'You're not taking him from me. Don't touch me.'

'Okay, okay. Please just stop walking for a minute. Jane, for God's sake.'

None of the passing cars stopped. For a while, it was just her walking with Daniel in her arms, Thomas close behind her, asking her to please stop. Then a siren sounded and Jane began to run. The siren stopped. But there were other footsteps now, along with Thomas's. An arm hard around her waist, and then a sharp pain in her thigh, like she'd been bitten.

She woke in a small hospital bedroom, her limbs too heavy to move. In a chair beside her bed, sat Thomas. He was holding Daniel. He was staring at her. He pressed a button and a nurse came in, shutting the door behind her.

'Awake. Good. How are you feeling, love? She's probably still a bit zonked.'

'I'm fine,' said Jane. 'I just want my child.'

Thomas looked at the nurse, then passed Daniel to Jane. He wriggled in her arms. He scrunched his face up and began to cry. He nuzzled her breast, his mouth opening and shutting like a fish. She tried to feed him but he got agitated, twisting his little body, trying, as usual, to get more milk than her body could produce.

'Do you have the formula?' she said to Thomas. She couldn't even look at him.

'Sure,' he said. 'I'll feed him, don't worry.' There was a look then, between Thomas and the nurse. They thought she didn't see it but she did.

The next day, they moved her to a mother and baby ward. Jane agreed to staying on in the hospital because she knew if she didn't they would take her baby off her forever. And when the psychiatrist came to see her, she knew better than to tell him what she really thought.

'How are you feeling today?' he asked her. He was a large man with a tired face.

'Fine,' she said.

'Do you know what happened yesterday?' He held her gaze.

'I just got a fright,' she said. She shook her head. 'It was nothing.'

'A fright. Can you remember what frightened you?'

Jane looked at her hands.

'Do you know where you are, Jane?'

'Hospital.'

'That's right. We're going to keep you here for a while until we find out what medicine will help.' He studied her a moment. 'We think you have something called postpartum psychosis. Have you ever heard of it?'

Jane looked out the window. A plastic bag was being whipped about in the air.

'Most people haven't. Look, it's serious, I won't lie, but I want you to remember two things okay? It's temporary, and it's treatable. Jane, can you look at me for a second?' He kept his gaze on her until she looked back.

'This must be frightening, but it'll pass. Okay? It will pass. Do you understand?'

She gave him a curt nod.

'Okay,' he said again, and left.

She was in that place for days, weeks. Every morning and every evening, a nurse gave her pills and stood by her bed until Jane swallowed them. Sometimes the shape or colour of them changed but the way Jane felt never did. Or if it did change, it was only to intensify, so that she found when she spoke, her words came out all jumbled up. This did not stop her talking. It became impossible, not to speak about the dangers. But no one would believe anything she said. Or else they would not admit what they knew. When she told the nurse and Thomas that their neighbour wanted to burn down their house, they said it was not true. When she told Thomas about the camera in the door of her room, he just shook his head.

She could not hold her baby anymore. She could not feed him. The pills they gave her would kill him. That was what they wanted. Everything was always too dangerous. Something terrible was going to happen and everyone was pretending they didn't know what she was talking about. One thing the drugs did do was make her sleep but the worst part was always waking up, her thoughts already fighting with the sluggishness, taking off against it.

One morning, a patient in another room began to scream. Jane watched the two nurses run down the hall and then she ran out of the ward. She ran down a flight of stairs, then another one. She got to an open window. She climbed onto the sill and looked up and down the corridor. She was alone. No one was going to stop her. She stepped out onto the ledge. She looked down. Three storeys, concrete ground below. She didn't know. Was this the answer? Was this what she was supposed to do? It felt as though it was.

Then hands, gripping her ankles. Urgent voices. An arm around her waist and the bite of a needle again. This time when she woke, Thomas was sitting by her bed. He looked like he'd been beaten. Already the thoughts were starting to gather and swirl inside her, even as she struggled to remember what had happened.

'What?' she said to him. 'What?'

'It has to end, Jane. The drugs aren't working fast enough.'

He wouldn't say anything else until the psychiatrist arrived. It was the same one as before, the one with the tired face. Sitting beside Thomas, he told her they wanted to try a different therapeutic approach. Called electroconvulsive therapy. It has a bad reputation, he said, but it can be very effective. We tend to get a much quicker response than we do with anti-depressants, or other medication, he said. And it's completely painless. The only side effect was memory loss, and that is usually temporary.

'I really think it's your best option,' he said, handing her a leaflet.

Jane looked at Thomas.

'For Daniel,' he said. 'He needs you. Please, Jane. I think it will help.'

It happened six times, the passing out and waking up to ache and nausea and not knowing anything. Slowly, her mind began to quieten. She stopped believing there was a camera in the door, or that their neighbour wanted to burn their house down. The feeling of some awful danger began to lose its grip. Memories were lost but most of them flitted back, old and new, in the days and weeks that followed.

For a long time, the guilt grew inside her, knotting up her stomach when she looked at Daniel and making it hard to breathe. But there was help. Her mother came and stayed with them, and there was a cleaner Thomas had taken on when she was in hospital. By then, Daniel was sleeping through most nights, so she did too. She started seeing a counsellor every Thursday, a white-haired woman who mostly just listened to Jane and who, when she said kind things, Jane believed.

One evening at the end of the autumn, Jane and Thomas went for a walk. It was the first time she passed their garden gate since the hospital. A hemline of orange where the sun had been was giving way to a darkening blue.

'Maybe it was selfish of me,' he said, after they'd been walking awhile. 'Bringing you all the way out here, then me going to work every day. You spent too much time on your own.'

'But I wanted it,' she said. 'I was happy.'

Back in the city, Jane joined a mother and baby group. She told them all, when they were introducing themselves and telling their stories, that she had had postpartum psychosis, but none of them ever asked her about it afterwards. And she got it, why they hadn't. What was there to say about it? Why dwell on something so negative? After that, she never brought it up if she could help it.

About a year later, she finally stopped taking the medication. She and Thomas began discussing the idea of her returning to work part-time. She got in touch with the library where she used to work. And once the guilt had abated (it never left entirely), and she had more or less recovered, all the delight returned. When he smiled at her or talked gobbledygook at her or even when he found it hilarious to bite her, or pull her hair or earrings, or when he was just sleeping, making his little sleep noises. She found him a good local crèche and that autumn, for three mornings a week, she started back in the library, on a part-time, temporary position. She would walk to the crèche, leave Daniel there, always with a tug of pain, and catch a bus to work. To her relief, she found she could perform her duties there without any huge difficulty. Sometimes, there was even a quiet kind of enjoyment. And then afterwards she got to walk through the doors of the crèche and breathe in her new favourite smell – a mixture of vegetable soup and nappy cream. Take him in her arms.

Life stayed tiring. There was no denying that. The mornings seemed to come around so quickly. Sometimes she felt as though she could sleep for a year. All mothers feel tired, of course, when their children are babies. She knew that. But she also knew that her tiredness contained an extra layer, borne out of her unwanted knowledge. That Jane's mind could break away from Jane, if it wanted to. That if Jane's mind ever did that again, it would want to win, just like it wanted to win the first time.

Even though she had known the answer, she still asked the psychiatrist at her last outpatient appointment with him. Yes, he had confirmed. It could come back, especially if she had another child, something she and Thomas had started to talk about. But we'll be prepared, he said, if that happens. You know better than I do how to survive it.

That evening, one of the lost memories presented itself. A sunny square in Italy, reading for hours while drinking too much coffee. Simply because she wanted to and because she could.

A desire rose inside her then – to warn that past self. But warn her of what? That woman was from a different world. Jane and not Jane. None of what had happened had anything to do with her.

The thing to do with that Jane was to let her go.

EUROPE

The voices of girls reached Karl as he approached the hostel. 'They came back with ginger beer and two bottles of vodka.'

'Are you serious?'

'They're gonna make punch in the sink.'

By the door he paused. There were two of them, both thin and tanned and good looking. One was swivelling herself around in her office chair in a lazy kind of way, the other sat on the desk, examining a strand of her long blonde hair.

'In the sink? Are they crazy?'

'Oh, they most definitely are crazy.'

Crazy. Crazy. He would just do it.

'I heard this was a party hostel,' he said, walking right up to that desk. He pushed his hair out of his eyes, and shrugged his rucksack from his shoulders so that it fell onto the ground, where it slumped sideways, one of the arms brushing against the blonde girl's leg. She stared at it.

'Sorry,' he said, lifting it up again.

'Can I help you?' said the one behind the desk.

'Oh sure,' he said. 'I'm Karl Burgess. Booked in for a couple of nights?'

She stared at her computer screen.

'Karl with a K. It's a dorm bed, I think?'

'Karl with a K.' She looked at the other girl who was still staring at him.

'You're on the top floor,' she finally said. 'Good luck getting any sleep there.'

'Is that where the guys are?'

'Yup.'

'That's no problem,' said Karl. 'I don't mind.'

'Okay. Well, enjoy your stay.' She handed over a key card.

'Thanks. Thanks a lot.' For a moment, Karl just stood there. Then he said it. 'So can anyone come to this party?'

'Oh,' said the one behind the desk. She looked at her friend again. 'I mean, it's no big deal. 'We'll just be out there.' And she looked behind her, at French doors, through which you could see a courtyard, a couple of picnic tables.

The blonde one was smiling at her nails.

'Sounds great,' Karl said.

The dorm had a sloped ceiling and three bunk beds crammed in.

It smelled of sweat and deodorant. A plastic bag, filled with what looked like dirty laundry, bulged in the middle of a tiled floor that was also strewn with sneakers and socks and a couple of empty water bottles.

Karl climbed the narrow, steel ladder to the only vacant bunk. For a while he sat there, cross-legged, looking at the ribbed fabric of his bag. The blonde girl's smile burned inside him. *Stupid, stupid*, he thought. *Stupid, stupid*. He could still feel the heat in his face. And now an ache was growing in his throat and he wanted, intensely, to speak to his mother. But instead he unzipped the top part of his rucksack and took out a notebook. In it he wrote the date and then, 'Today I arrived in Europe. First stop: Florence, Italy. Just got to the hostel. Have been invited to a party tonight'. It was an idea he'd gotten from a self-help book. A journal where you only record the good things. It was supposed to change the way you felt, until you only ever felt good. Fake it till you make it. He'd started it the day he'd handed in his notice in the bar and then gone home to tell his mother he'd failed his exams.

'I guess it's simple. I guess I'm too dumb for medicine,' he'd said, trying to laugh again. He could not look at her.

'You're not *dumb*.' Her mouth was slightly open as she stared at him. 'That's not what the problem is.'

The bar had been terrible. Long hours polishing tables and glasses just to look busy, while the others chatted to the regulars with ease.

'You have to help me out here.' She screwed her eyes at him and the old heaviness came – like the blood in his veins had been replaced with some other, weightier substance.

'I'd ask if there was a girl, but.'

'No girl. I just screwed up. On my own.'

What was it that girl he slept with had said to him when he had been complaining about college? *So what do you want to do?* He had not been able to answer her. He could not tell her the truth – it would be too strange – that for as long as he could remember, there had never been anything he had wanted to do.

'Well, how am I supposed to understand? He won't talk to me,' said his mother. 'You can repeat them, right?'

'August.'

She stared ahead of her. He could almost hear her figure it out – how he would spend the summer there with her, every day studying. In August, he would take the repeats. And then he would go back to college.

After a shower, Karl left the hostel and walked the yellow, baking city without once looking at his map. He did not read the inscription of a single statue or peer inside the cool of a church. He did not pause to find out why a long queue of tourists ran all the way down a street and curled itself around a corner. He did not even stop to take in the fat, brown river that sludged through the city, or its shop-lined bridge. Only when he came to a piazza cluttered with people and English-language menus did he stop walking and realise how tired he was. How much he could do with a drink.

It was pleasant to take a table under the shade of an awning and order a beer and a pizza. So what if it cost a whole day's budget.

It was his first day. He needed to give himself a chance to settle in. He'd arrived in Europe after all. Half a world away.

Like a good omen, there came then a warm, melodic tune. Karl turned to see a woman playing a violin. The word willowy came to him as he took her in, in her black jeans and t-shirt. As he watched, a person dropped a coin into her case, and she smiled her thanks at them, all the while her fingers continuing their back and forth darting on the neck of her instrument. Karl took out his notebook again, and turned to a marked page, the one with the quotations. *The definition of insanity,* read the first one, *is doing the same thing over and over and expecting a different result.*

When his third beer came, he downed it quickly and put his money on the table. As soon as she stopped and people began wandering away, he walked right up to her. Then he took the last five euro note from his wallet and dropped it into the case, where it lay upon the coins.

'Molto grazie,' she said, smiling at him.

He could see a tiny freckle under her right eye, how the sides of her fringe were wet and clung to her forehead.

'Great music,' he said. 'Thank *you.*' He squinted out into the square. 'I don't suppose you want to get a coffee?'

'Ah. No, I cannot. I must continue.' She gestured with her violin. She smiled.

'Maybe later? I can wait.'

'No, no. Thank you.' She glanced around her. 'Goodbye,' she smiled. But then she was looking behind him. And when Karl turned around, there was a man standing there. It was the waiter from the café.

'You do not leave enough money,' he said.

'Sorry?'

The waiter held up a twenty euro note. 'One pizza, three beer. Four more please.'

'I forgot the third beer.' He opened his wallet. It was empty. 'I can go get more. What about my card? Do you take credit card?'

'It's okay,' said the violin player. She had already taken the five euro note from her case and now handed it to the waiter.

'Grazie, signora,' he said, and he and the violin player began talking, rapidly it seemed to Karl, in Italian.

'Thanks,' he said to the violin player but she just kept on talking to the waiter.

On the other side of the piazza, a man shouted at him.

'Care! Care, please.' Gesturing at Karl's feet.

Looking down, Karl realised the problem; he was standing on the sheet displaying the man's fake designer bags.

'Sorry,' he said.

He did not know exactly where he was walking; vaguely it felt it was in the direction of the hostel, down this street and then that one. On one he passed a small supermarket; he doubled back and went inside it and with his credit card bought two bottles of red wine. Back outside, refreshed a little by the air conditioning, he decided he would walk until he found a little park or even a street bench. But before he came upon either he found himself back on the street where the hostel was. So he just hunkered down in the shade, and necked one of the bottles. A sharp headache was uncoiling itself but he kept drinking, even when a couple walking past stared at him, and a young man on a Vespa seemed to slow down to take in the sight of him.

Back at the hostel, he passed people clustered around the desk and made straight for the French doors, pushing them open. He hadn't meant to slam them like that. A couple of people looked his way. But among them he saw the two girls from earlier. They were sitting at one of the tables.

'Hey there,' he said, sitting beside the one who had checked him in.

'Oh. Hello. How are you?'

The blonde one turned and stared at him.

'Great,' he said.

'That's good. Enjoying the city.'

'Oh, it's an amazing city.'

Then he kept talking. He told her about how he was using up his college loan for his trip. How that didn't matter because on this trip everything was going to change. He told her he was actually glad the two guys from college had changed their minds about going in the end. Truth be told, his college wasn't the kind of place you could make friends too easily. Then there was his mother who thought he should be spending the summer with her, studying for his repeats. It was time for a change, that's all he knew. Like coming here on his own – he didn't even think about it, he just booked the flights and this hostel and that was it. He was just going to wing the rest of it.

'Wow,' said the blonde girl when he finally paused and Karl became aware of the unblinking stare of a tall guy standing on the other side of the table, a beer bottle in his hand. But he had to keep going, because if he stopped talking, they would all go away and there he would be, a thousand miles from home on his own in the middle of a party, surrounded by people sitting on each other or kneeling on the ground, just to be together. Soon he would be like that too, this trip was going to bring it out of him. He might even decide to live in Europe, get a job in Paris or somewhere like that. That's what he told them next and he would have kept talking if there hadn't suddenly come a loud thudding sound, which had everyone look towards the French doors. Then it happened again: the loud thud, a shout, laughter. This time, Karl thought he saw something dark briefly press against the French door.

'What the hell is that?' shouted the beer bottle guy.

'A fucking cat, man,' shouted someone from behind the door. 'It can't see the fucking glass, keeps trying to go through it.'

It happened again, and again, until finally someone went to the door and opened it and a black cat shot across the courtyard and over the wall. A last clatter of laughter, a couple of whoops, then the two girls went inside and the beer bottle guy followed.

Back in the dorm room, Karl sat on his bunk, every couple of minutes necking some wine. Though the window was closed, he could still hear the party continue below. When he'd finished the bottle, he went back downstairs, where the girls and the beer bottle guy and a couple of others were sitting at the same table.

'Come on,' the beer bottle guy was saying. No one seemed to notice Karl joining them again.

'No way,' said someone else. 'You're fucking crazy.'

Karl picked up a packet of matches on the table, just to have something to do. First he turned it over and over in his hands. Then he did his party trick – balancing five matches between his fingers, and then lifting them over his head and back to the table. As he was doing it, eyes closed, the talking stopped. He could feel them watching.

'Hey, hey,' said the beer bottle guy, after Karl had put the matches on the box, one by one, in a neat little row. 'I bet this guy could do it.'

'Do what?'

'Nothing,' said the girl that had booked him in. 'Don't listen to him, he's an idiot.'

But the beer bottle guy was still looking at Karl. 'There's this pool? On the roof of the house across the lane?' he said. 'You know that tiny little lane? And there's this roof garden thing on the top of our building? A quick jump over and like you can actually get across to the pool.'

'It's a total cinch,' said another guy.

'It's dangerous,' said the girl.

'I've done it twice already.'

'Don't listen to him.'

'Who's coming? Come on, it'll be a riot.'

The beer bottle guy was standing now. The others were looking at him, but none of them stood.

'I'm on the high jump team at college,' lied Karl. 'I guess I could give it a go.'

'Alright,' shouted the beer bottle guy, coming around and high fiving him.

Up on the roof, a purple sky held a thin scattering of stars. The horizon was a sliver of pale gold. Beneath, among the higgledy-piggledy rust-red rooftops, a huge dome stood startlingly close, its pale chequered marble a shock of beauty. And all around, the silhouette of other domes and steeples and towers stood silent and lovely, as though, it seemed to Karl, dimly, that they were waiting for something and would wait forever.

No lamp lit the narrow alley between their building and the one with the pool, and the ground below lay in darkness. Karl could just about see the part of the other roof that they had to jump onto.

'I'll just do it,' said beer bottle guy, and then, more suddenly than Karl had anticipated, he was taking a leaping step across the night. And then he was waving at them from across the way.

'Piece of cake,' he shouted. 'Who's next?'

The blonde girl looked like she was bracing herself but then her face changed and she looked at Karl.

'Well, Karl with a K?' she said.

There was no room to build up much of a run. It was simply a matter of taking two running steps and then launching yourself into the air. It was a very short distance. Karl took two steps back, two forward, and then he hesitated – for a bare moment, but it seemed, in that minute fraction of time, with all those faces on him, impossible not to take a third step, even though in that brief pause he had lost some tiny, essential momentum.

When Karl's torso hit the slates, all that mattered was that his arms were pressing hard down onto the roof and that beer bottle guy was already scrambling towards him. He didn't feel any pain.

Before the eave creaked and gave way and he was falling, it had only been a matter of hanging on.

IN KALAMAZOO

When Sofia and her granddad passed through the archway and into the square, everything was under one big shadow. Even though the sky was blue and later the sun would be in it, shining down on everything. Sofia's hand felt hot inside her granddad's, and he was walking along like he didn't care if the rest of her came with it. She had to run sometimes, to keep up with him. They had walked like this all the way from the street where they lived, she in her house with her parents, he in his apartment on the other side.

By the carousel, she kept her feet together. She made a fist so that when he kept walking, her hand slipped out of his.

'You're walking too fast for me, Nono,' she said, and she yawned.

But her granddad just looked at her, like he couldn't understand the words. Sofia rubbed her eyes and a hard bit scratched out of one of them.

'Ah,' he said then. 'Silly old Nono.'

His hair stood out from his head on one side. His eyes were pink at the edges. Half his shirt hung over his trousers, and it looked like the shirt he had been wearing the day before.

'You look weird,' she said.

Again he looked at her, as though he did not understand.

'Where are we going?'

'I told you,' he said. 'For a walk. For a little breakfast.'

Sofia only ever had breakfast at home. But this morning, the biscuit tin had stayed closed on the shelf. And her mother had not been in the kitchen. She had been outside, in her dressing gown with Aunt Elena. She had gotten into Aunt Elena's car and they had driven away.

'Where was Mama going this morning?' she asked again.

'She has a cold. Aunt Elena's looking after her today. Remember?'

Yesterday, Sofia's mother had worked in the garden as Sofia played with her dolls. She had been singing.

'She never leaves that early.'

'Elena had to open her shop. Now let's go.'

Sofia looked at the carousel. 'What's the yellow cover for?'

'The horses,' he said. 'They're still asleep. Lazy old horses.'

Sofia walked over and tried to lift it. But it was heavy and had dirt on the edges you could only see up close. It slipped against her fingers. And then she saw, on the other side, there was a man leaning against a wall and watching her. He had a long beard, and long hair that looked like no one ever brushed.

Sofia ran back to her granddad.

'There's a man,' she said.

'Don't mind him,' said her granddad. 'He's just a bum.'

'What's a bum?'

'Someone who doesn't care about anything.' He didn't look at her as he spoke and he sounded annoyed, even as he took her hand and they began to walk again, more slowly this time, through the square, up Via della Speziali and into a coffee shop, where a woman was turning chairs from tables onto the floor.

'I want that,' she said, pointing to a huge, dark chocolate cake on the counter. Her granddad only nodded. And when she was eating her thick slice, he said nothing when she got crumbs on the table top and floor, not even when she pushed large pieces into her mouth. He just looked at his phone, or out the window.

'Papa was shouting last night,' she said.

Only then did his eyes pull back to her. He looked frightened.

'I told him to turn down that TV,' he said.

'Where was he this morning?'

'Your father's at work.'

'He's very busy.'

'That's right'. He looked at her again and this time, his face changed. 'The best girl in Florence,' he said. He put his huge hand on her head.

'You stink, Nono,' she said, pinching her nose with her fingers. 'We should go home so you can have a shower.'

He laughed then. And back outside, he said some of the English words he had learned in the war, when he stayed with the Americans.

'Less go boys. You wan some ice cream? Sunuvabitch.' He said them in the voice that made Sofia laugh. Then she asked what happens in a war. It was a game they had.

'Some people fight,' he said. 'Then to cheer themselves up, some people sing happy songs.' And he lifted her up onto his shoulders and began to sing. She joined in at the end.

'I've got a gal in Kalamazoo/Don't want to boast but I know she's the toast of Kalamazoo/Zoo, Zoo, Zoo, Zoo, Zoo.'

'That's it,' he said. 'We'll go to the zoo in Pistoia.'

'Can we take the train?' she said.

'Why not?'

'But. First, let's go home and check on our tomatoes. There were two more yesterday.'

'You know your mama told me we should have fun today? And come back when she's all better?'

'She said that?'

'Absolutely.'

At the zoo, they saw insects that looked just like the twigs they held onto. Sofia's granddad said they made themselves that way so no one could see them. They saw wolf cubs. It looked like they were trying to hurt each other but her granddad told her that that was how wolf cubs play. Birds screeched from trees. A sow lay on the ground, with a row of piglets sucking milk from her teats. It looked sore the way they pulled at them, but the sow just lay there, looking up at Sofia.

Sometimes, when she asked her granddad a question, he didn't hear her and she had to say it again. Over and over, he took his phone from his pocket and looked at it and put it back.

In the restaurant, he bought them big plates of French fries and glasses of Coca Cola.

'Papa doesn't go to work on a Saturday,' she said, when they had found a table. 'He does his work at home, in the office.'

'He does?'

Sofia nodded. Her grandfather knew that already.

'Well, it's like you said, he's very busy.' And he tapped the table top with his fingers, looked around the restaurant.

'Very busy, very busy, very busy.' She pushed four French fries into her mouth. She looked around the room, at the children and their parents eating and talking and banging their plates and babies crying.

'Take it easy, Sofia,' he said, in a loud voice. Then he smiled at her strangely. 'Let's see some more animals,' he said. 'But first, I've to make a quick phone call. Don't go anywhere, okay?'

Once he was by the door, three tables away, and talking on his phone, his back to her, it was easy to cross the room and crouch into the orange plastic seat behind him.

'That's what I mean,' he was saying. 'How is she now?' And Sofia knew he was talking about her mother. Then he said, 'He got an order on Lucca? But you know what he'll do now? He'll go home. That's what that bastard will do.'

Sofia had never heard her granddad use that word before. But she kept listening. She wanted to know what else he might say about her father.

'I'll keep Sofia with me until tomorrow,' he said. 'Oh, she's okay. I think.'

He turned then, before she could move.

'How long have you been there?'

'A second.'

'Did you hear me talking?'

'No.'

When they left the zoo, Sofia said her feet were tired, so he carried her on his shoulders again, back into the town of Pistoia, where he got them ice creams. As they ate, they walked the streets and Sofia's granddad told her stories about some of the people in the houses they passed. The woman in that one, he said, has a pair of blue boots. Whenever she wears them, she goes invisible. The man who lives there can't stop whistling. A witch put a spell on him. Sofia said nothing. She knew it was all made up. And later, on the train, she rested her head against the window and closed her eyes. She kept them closed all the way in the train and in the taxi and when her granddad lay her on the bed in his spare room. She did not open them again until she could hear the television.

From the hallway, she could see him sitting on the sofa. She could see the white hair on the back of his head and his hand on the arm of the chair.

Quietly, she walked down the hall and out the door, pressed the button and took the elevator on her own. She pushed open the tall, dark door of the apartment building and stepped outside. The street was quiet. Although there was still blue in the sky, the lamps were on. Across the road, her home, the house she lived in with her mother and father, was dark and all the shutters were closed. Sometimes Sofia's parents went out at night time and then Amelia Lucca looked after her. Amelia Lucca was beautiful, and nearly finished school. When Sofia grew up, she was going to wear earrings just like hers.

But now, there was no Amelia. Sofia ran across the road, and up to her front door. She put her finger on the doorbell and kept it there. Then footsteps were in the hall. The door opened and her father was there, staring down at her.

'Papa,' she said. She took a step towards him. She lifted her arms. But he said nothing. He just looked down at her, like he was trying to remember who she was. His shirt was open so she could see the dark hair inside it. The bottom half of his face was dark too. She thought of the man in the square that morning.

'Sofia,' he said then. Like he had just found the word. And he lifted her and held her against his chest. He took a step backwards, leaned against the wall. 'My little Sofia. You're on my side, aren't you? You came to cheer me up.' But the words came out all joined together. His fingers pinched. A mean smell came from his mouth.

'You're hurting me,' she said.

His hands went loose and she slid to the floor. He looked at her like she had done something wrong.

'Always with the tears,' he said. 'A spoiled little girl. Here's a gift for you, spoiled Sofia. How would you like Amelia to have a little brother for you? You'd like that maybe. To play with.' He laughed, but it sounded ugly. Then he turned around, walked down the hall-way. He knocked himself against the wall on his way, like he could not see, even though the light was on. Sofia followed him.

'Amelia can't have a brother for me,' she said. 'Only Mama.'

But he just laughed again. 'This is great news you bring me, Sofia,' he said. 'All my troubles have gone away.'

He fell onto the sofa. Then he closed his eyes. From outside, she heard her granddad calling her name, loudly, over and over.

Two stars were in the navy sky. There was no moon. A cricket called out and waited for another one to call back. All the hedges and plants were still and dark, and it felt like they were watching her. She walked past the flower bed, where yesterday her mother had weeded, past the grape vines, and down to the vegetables at the end. Heads of lettuce snuggled against the ground. Basil plants sat fat and leafy. And behind them, the tomato plants stood still in a row.

It wasn't hard to pull the unripe tomatoes from each plant. Some of them were tiny and some had grown quite big, but they all came loose with only a small tug. When she was finished, the pile of them was bigger than her two hands put together.

But she didn't know of the idea of eating them until the first one was in her mouth. It was a small one, its skin tight against its hard insides. She bit down and her mouth filled with the sharp, awful taste. It seemed all her body wanted was to get it out. She kept chew-ing and then she swallowed. And when, seconds later, pain sprang up in her stomach, she put a second, bigger one in her mouth and bit down hard.

PIAZZA DELLA REPUBBLICA

This square bristles with people. Among the restaurant tables that clutter it, waiters weave like swallows. Fake wears – sunglasses, handbags, t-shirts – lined out on rugs along the edge form a lively border. Tourists inspect, sellers watch. At the far side, a dense crowd gathers around a Charlie Chaplin impersonator. Closer by, a policewoman argues with a woman carrying a pile of glistening scarves on her shoulder. The policewoman does most of the talking and her arm movements suggest exasperation. The other woman's weapon is silence and she seems to be winning.

Padraig is stirring his coffee. He does it as though the act is a novel one. This is because she and he are in love, and because it is ridiculous for them to feel this way. They have spent the whole afternoon in her bedroom, a day's itinerary abandoned.

The warmth of the day has been stored up by the square and it feels like sitting in a warm bath, even though the sun has set and without the electric lights they would be in complete darkness. This evening, in the rush to make their dinner reservation, he forgot to put on aftershave and Emily is glad of this. He is sitting close enough for her to smell him. His scent is warm and salty and makes her want to lick his cheek. It is a startling image that draws heat to her face. He glances at her, casually places his arm along the back of her chair, like a teenager at the cinema.

All around them the dance of the square continues. On her first night in this city, someone told her that a Jewish quarter once bustled there. It was razed to the ground in the nineteenth century in order to give Florence a grand central point. Homes and a market, which must have been the centre of a whole community, destroyed. Probably in a matter of days. The place was for others now, to draw their stories through. Emily wonders what all this life is for, what it is climbing towards. She can't tell. She doesn't think she will ever be able to tell.

She turns to the man beside her, skirts the back of her fingers across his forehead, down the side of his face.

ACKNOWLEDGEMENTS

Thanks are due to the editors of the following magazines, where some of these stories appeared: *Confrontation Magazine* (The Strangler Tree), *Mslexia* (None Of Us Will Be Okay), *The Manchester Review* (Colette Went Quiet) and *LITRO* (In Kalamazoo). I am also grateful to Seamus Hosey, then producer of the RTÉ Radio 1 Francis MacManus Short Story Award programme, for his radio production of None Of Us Will Be Okay.

Thanks to the members of my old writing group – Deirdre Leahy, Olivia Morahan, Liz O'Neill and Siobhán Mannion – for their generous attention and valuable feedback on drafts of many of these stories. To members of the Liz Lehrman writing workshop who shared their views, a sincere thank you to you as well. Over the years, I have been lucky enough to attend fiction writing workshops facilitated by Claire Keegan, where drafts of some of these stories were critiqued. Any insights I gained there, on fiction and on writing it, are to me worth their weight in gold.

Emma O'Donoghue, thank you for our book conversations! Which I find so nurturing. I hope there are many more to come.

I am so grateful to Aaron Kent and Alice Brooker and everyone else in Broken Sleep Books who took a punt on this little collection so that now these stories finally get to live together.

Last but not least, thanks are due to the members of my own household – my husband John, my children Martha and Brendan, and our springer spaniel, Biscuit.

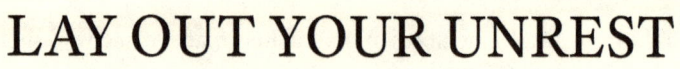

LAY OUT YOUR UNREST